# WELCOME TO

# Beast Quest ®

Collect the special coins in this book.
You will earn one gold coin for
every chapter you read.

Once you have finished all the chapters,
find out what to do with your gold coins at
the back of the book.

With special thanks to Stephen Cole

*For Jamie Morgan*

www.beastquest.co.uk

ORCHARD BOOKS
Carmelite House
50 Victoria Embankment
London EC4Y 0DZ

A Paperback Original
First published in Great Britain in 2007
This edition published in 2015

Beast Quest is a registered trademark of Beast Quest Limited
Series created by Beast Quest Limited, London

A CIP catalogue record for this book is available from
the British Library.

ISBN 978 1 40834 763 8

1

Printed and bound by CPI Group (UK) Ltd, Croydon, CR0 4YY

The paper and board used in this book are made from wood
from responsible sources.

Orchard Books
An imprint of Hachette Children's Group
Part of The Watts Publishing Group Limited
An Hachette UK Company

www.hachette.co.uk

# Beast Quest

# FERNO
## THE FIRE
## DRAGON

### BY ADAM BLADE

ORCHARD

THE ICY

THE NORTHERN
MOUNTAINS

WESTERN OCEAN

THE FOREST
OF FEAR

# CONTENTS

*Welcome to the Kingdom of Avantia. I am Aduro – a Good Wizard residing in the palace of King Hugo. You join us at a difficult time. Let me explain...*

*The Ancient Scripts say that our peaceful kingdom shall one day be plunged into peril.*

*Now that time has come.*

*Under the evil spell of Malvel the Dark Wizard, six Beasts – fire dragon, sea serpent, mountain giant, horse-man, snow monster and flame bird – run wild and destroy the land they once protected.*

*Avantia is in danger, but the Ancient Scripts also predict an unlikely hero. It is written that a boy shall take up the Quest to free the Beasts from the curse and save the kingdom.*

*We do not know who this boy is, only that his time has come...*

*We pray our young hero will have the courage and the heart to take up the Quest. Will you join us as we wait and watch?*

*Avantia salutes you,*

*Aduro*

# PROLOGUE

Caldor the Brave stood at the
foot of the mountain. His bronze
armour gleamed in the pale morning
sunlight.

"The fire dragon is close. I can feel
it." The knight pointed his sword
up towards the mist at the top of
the mountain. "For the sake of our
kingdom, it must be stopped!"

"Good luck, sir," said Edward,

his young page.

Caldor held out an armoured hand and placed it on Edward's shoulder. They both understood that they might never see each other again.

The knight turned to climb the smooth, dark slope. His feet slipped and skidded on the rock. But he dragged himself up with determination, slowly climbing higher and higher. Soon the mist closed behind him and he was lost from sight.

All that was left was an eerie silence. Edward shivered. Suddenly the mountain started to shake.

Edward could feel the vibrations travelling through his feet and up his legs. He stumbled and his chin hit the ground as a huge judder threw him to the ground. There was a metallic taste in his mouth. *Blood!*

What was happening?

"Caldor!" Edward yelled, scrambling to his feet as the rocks shifted beneath him. "Come back!"

But his voice was lost in the grinding sounds that filled the air. The whole mountain shook violently. Was it about to come crashing down on him?

Edward was seized with panic. Heart pounding, he looked up and saw two overhanging rocks start to move. Their sharp edges caught the light as they edged out. Suddenly, they slashed through the air like giant axe-heads. Edward flinched.

As the mist cleared, he glimpsed Caldor clinging to the side of the mountain. Then something reared up beyond the knight, and Edward saw the flash of an eye and the thick scales of leathery skin. It was the spiked head of a huge dragon!

Suddenly everything made horrible sense. His master had been right. The Beast was close. This wasn't a mountain...it was the dragon itself! Glancing down with a rush of fear, Edward realised that he was standing on the dragon's tail – and that Caldor was holding onto the monster's back! And those two overhanging rocks were the dragon's mighty wings. He wanted to run, but his legs were frozen with fear.

Now he could see the sides of the dragon moving in and out as it breathed heavily. Steam hissed out of the creature's nostrils.

"Caldor, come back!" Edward yelled again. But a terrifying roar drowned out his words.

The dragon's wings unfolded again, stretching out to beat the air in a deadly rhythm.

"It's taking off!" Edward shouted. "Caldor, quick—"

"Get back!" Caldor's words carried faintly on the air. "Go to the city. Warn King Hugo. Run!"

Before Edward could move, the dragon flicked its tail, sending him flying. He hit the ground hard, shaking and gasping for breath, as the terrifying Beast rose up into the air. Caldor's screams filled his head.

Edward struggled to his feet and tried to run after his master, but the dragon was already high above him. It let out a huge roar, and a jet of orange flame lit up the sky. As it disappeared into the distance, one of Caldor's gauntlets, scorched and smoking, clattered to the ground beside Edward. Clutched in its fingers was a golden key.

The echoes of Caldor's cries hung in the air. Then, silence. The knight was gone.

And his mission to free the fire dragon from Malvel's terrible curse had failed.

# THE MYSTERIOUS FIRE

Tom stared hard at his enemy. "Surrender, villain," he cried, "or taste my blade!"

He gave the sack of hay a blow with the poker. "That's you taken care of," he announced. "One day I'll be the finest swordsman in all Avantia. Even better than my father, Taladon the Swift!"

Tom felt the ache in his heart that

always came when he thought about his father. The uncle and aunt who had brought Tom up since he was a baby never spoke about him or why he had left Tom to their care after Tom's mother had died.

He shoved the poker back into his pack. "One day I'll know the truth," he swore.

As Tom walked back to the village, a sharp smell caught at the back of his throat.

*Smoke!* he thought.

He stopped and looked around. Through the trees to his left, he could hear a faint crackling as a wave of warm air hit him.

*Fire!*

Tom pushed his way through the

trees and burst into a field. The golden wheat had been burned to black stubble and a veil of smoke hung in the air. Tom stared in horror. How could this have happened?

He looked up and blinked. For a second he thought he saw a dark shape moving towards the hills in the distance. But then the sky was empty once again.

An angry voice called out. "Who's there?"

Through the smoke, Tom saw a figure stamping round the edge of the field.

"Did you come through the woods?" the man demanded. "Did you see who did this?"

Tom shook his head. "I didn't see a soul!"

"There's evil at work here," said the farmer, his eyes flashing. "Go and tell your uncle what's happened. Our village of Errinel is cursed – and maybe all of us with it!"

Tom turned and ran as fast as he could, stumbling over the blackened tree roots.

Tom burst into the village square, gasping for breath. It was full of villagers. What were they all doing here? It wasn't market day. They were shouting and waving their hands at his uncle, who was standing on a bench at the edge of the square.

"Fire in the fields! What next?" one man shouted.

"The troubles get worse each day!" called another villager.

"The Beasts have turned evil!"

Tom knew that Avantia was said to be protected by six Beasts, including a fire dragon, but no one was sure if they really existed.

"Have you seen the river?" a woman asked. "It's so low we will soon run out of drinking water."

"We're cursed," an old man wailed.

"I don't believe in curses," said Tom's uncle firmly. "But our village needs help. One of us must go to the king and request his aid."

Tom stepped forward. "*I'll* go to the palace, Uncle."

The villagers laughed. "Send a boy on such a mission? Ha!"

"The king would laugh at us for sending a child."

Tom's uncle spoke quietly. "No, Tom. You're too young. I'm head of the village. I'll go."

Suddenly a small boy, smeared in soot, pushed through the crowd. "Help!" he gasped. "Please help! Our barn is on fire!"

"Men! Bring your pails to the river now!"Tom's uncle roared to the crowd. "The rest of you bring spades to the barn – if we can't quench the fire we'll bury it. Quickly!"

Tom looked at his uncle as the men rushed to obey. "The village needs you here as its leader, Uncle Henry," he said. "Please let me go instead."

Tom's uncle turned to face him, his face serious. "I suppose I have to let you out into the world sooner or later," he said. He stared into the distance. "Perhaps it's meant to be..." He shook himself and turned back to Tom. "Yes, you must go to the king. And there is no time to waste – you will have to leave first thing tomorrow!"

1

# 2

# JOURNEY TO THE CITY

It was dark when Tom began his journey. But as the sun rose, he saw that Errinel wasn't the only place in trouble. As he strode further away from the village, he passed countless fields that had been scorched black. Alongside them, dry ditches traced paths where streams had once flowed.

He kept walking through the morning and into the afternoon, ignoring his tired muscles and aching feet. As he drew nearer the city, other people joined him on the dusty road. Horsemen cantered past and donkeys weighed down with packs trudged along steadily, driven on by families walking beside them. He could hear people muttering to each other. They seemed to be fleeing famine and danger. Clearly, he wasn't the only one heading to the palace to ask for help. Tom started to walk faster.

The towering city gates stood before him at last. They were wide open. As he passed through them, Tom felt a new surge of energy. He was here at last! He pushed his way through the narrow, crowded streets. He had one aim – and that was to get to the palace as quickly as possible. He could see it up ahead. It dwarfed all the other buildings with its purple spires and domes of sea-green glass. Tom had never seen anything like it!

But as he stepped through the main gateway into the palace courtyard he groaned. In front of him was a long line of people, and it was barely moving.

"Here to see the king's clerk?" a soldier asked Tom.

"No, I'm here to see the king!" Tom told him.

The soldier laughed. "You'll have

to see the king's clerk first. It's up to him who sees the king. Stand in line. You've a long wait."

"I can't wait here!" Tom said. "My village needs help – fast!"

"All of us need help," retorted a stout man with a beard that reached down to his knees. "In the West we've been hit by tidal waves. We need to build sea-barriers, but we can't do it without help from the king!"

"There are terrible blizzards in the North," said an old woman. "The whole kingdom is in danger! And mark my words – the Beasts have done this."

"The Beasts?" scoffed the stout man. "You must be joking!"

The woman glared at him angrily. "If no one believes in the Beasts, how will they ever be stopped? Something has happened to turn them against us. Yes, something evil has disturbed the Beasts..."

"What do you mean?" Tom asked.

But the woman turned her back on him and walked away.

Tom found himself thinking of the dark shape he had glimpsed amongst the hills back in Errinel. Could that figure have been a Beast? Could it have been the fire dragon? Tom looked at the long line of people in front of him again and made up his mind. He'd come to ask the king for help, and that was exactly what he was going to do –

even if it meant breaking into the
palace. "While there's blood in my
veins," he swore, "I'm going to save
my village!" He pushed his way
back through the crowds and out of
the palace courtyard.

When night had fallen, Tom started to circle the palace walls. Pale moonlight shone down upon him. "What I need is an open window," he muttered under his breath. "Or an unlocked door."

But guards were posted all the way round the palace. Tom crept towards the eastern gateway, but it was manned by two burly men in brown uniforms.

Suddenly there was the sound of running footsteps behind Tom. A ragged lad stumbled out of the dark night.

"Open the gates!" the boy shouted hoarsely. He was around Tom's age, and was covered in dirt. In one hand he clutched a blackened gauntlet and in the other a parchment scroll. "I bring word from Sir Caldor. I must see the king!"

The guards opened the gates, leaving them ajar, and ran to help the boy. Tom felt a thrill of hope run through his body.

Fortune was on his side.

*This is it,* he thought. *This is my chance to save Errinel!*

# THE KING'S COURT

Tom sprinted through the gateway while the guards' backs were turned, and hid in the shadows by the wall, edging his way round the courtyard. The smell of roasting meat wafted across from an open door. His stomach growled loudly.

"The palace kitchens must be through there," he said to himself. "If I go in, maybe I'll find a way of getting to the king."

As soon as Tom walked through the door, he was struck by heat so fierce it reminded him of his uncle's forge back in Errinel. Huge iron cauldrons hung over open fires. Kitchen maids milled about, stirring the stew or laying out food on silver platters.

A large woman bustled up to him. "Ah, at last!" she cried. "You must be the new kitchen boy."

"What? Oh yes, that's right," Tom agreed quickly.

"I'm Cook," the woman continued. "Thank goodness you're here to help! I've got two serving girls off sick and the king's supper is almost ready. You can take him what little food we have left."

Tom couldn't believe the palace was short of food. The kingdom's troubles were even worse than he had imagined.

Tom followed Cook to where platters of food waited, ready for serving. A steward gave Tom a quick lesson in balancing a platter on one hand held high above his head. Then he led Tom and the other servants up to the royal dining chamber.

Tom's heart beat fast. There, seated at a long table lit by tall candles, was King Hugo. He looked younger than Tom had imagined, with thick dark hair and large brown eyes. He was surrounded by grim-faced lords and ladies. Squaring his shoulders, Tom carried his platter to the far end of the table. "I have to talk to the king," he told himself. "Errinel is relying on me."

Next to the king sat a short, elderly man with a wispy beard. He was dressed in a gown of faded blue and red silk, with a pointed hat perched on his head. The old man's grey eyes seemed to glow in the candlelight, as brightly as the jewel he wore on a chain around his neck.

*Isn't it only wizards who dress like that?* Tom thought.

"Well, messengers would look pretty stupid in these clothes, wouldn't they?" said the old man with a smile.

Tom gasped. "You read my mind!"

"That's because I *am* a wizard.

Wizard Aduro," the old man murmured, looking closely at Tom. "But what are *you*, I wonder...?"

Just then the dining chamber doors flew open. The ragged young boy Tom had seen at the gates scrambled inside. Two guards followed closely behind him.

"Forgive me, sire," the boy cried. He sank to his knees before the king and held out the scorched gauntlet. Tom noticed that a golden key was clutched in its fingers. "I am Edward, page to Caldor the Brave. My master is dead."

"Dead!" echoed the king, jumping to his feet. He leaned forward, his knuckles turning white as he gripped the edge of the table. "It cannot be!"

"It is true, sire." The boy's eyes
brimmed with tears. "He's been
burned to death by the fire dragon,
Ferno. Our Quest is over."

Tom could hardly believe his ears.
So the Beasts *were* real!

King Hugo turned to stare out of a
window carved into the thick walls

of the castle. Through the window, Tom could see the city stretching far out into the night, its lights twinkling. "My bravest knight has perished," the king cried in despair. "Avantia is doomed!"

Wizard Aduro walked to the centre of the room. His face was grave, but he seemed calm. "The king's council has urgent matters to discuss," he announced. "I must ask all servants to leave us at once."

Escorted by two guards, the serving staff left the dining room, murmuring as they went.

*I'm not going!* Tom thought. This was his chance to find out exactly what was going on.

"Hurry up there!" the guards

ordered, pushing past Tom as the last stragglers left the room.

Thinking quickly, Tom doubled back to hide behind a large pillar near the king's chair. He pressed his cheek against the cold stone. His heart was thumping so loudly that he was sure someone would hear it.

"Curse the Dark Wizard Malvel!" cried one lord. "We *must* break this evil spell he has placed upon the Beasts, before the fire dragon, Ferno, destroys us all!"

*An evil spell!* Tom gasped loudly, then slapped a hand over his mouth.

Edward the page whipped around. "Who's that in the shadows?"

"A spy!" exclaimed King Hugo.

"Please, let me explain!" Tom

begged as two guards lunged towards him. He dodged out of the way, but a third threw himself at Tom's legs. Tom leapt over him and cried out to the king, "I'm only here because I want to save lives!" The guards grabbed him by the arms.

"Enough!" thundered Wizard Aduro, and everybody froze.

"Take him to the dungeons," ordered King Hugo, walking towards Tom. He gazed down at him.

Tom had never looked into the eyes of a king before. He bowed his head.

"Away!" King Hugo called, waving a hand towards the doors. "Take him away."

Just then Aduro appeared at the king's side. "This boy is here for a good reason. I can feel it."

The guards stopped in their tracks.

"Are you sure?" King Hugo asked after a long pause.

Aduro pointed at Tom. "Can't you see the likeness?" he asked.

King Hugo peered at Tom, then shook his head.

Tom blinked. *The likeness?* What was Aduro talking about?

Once again the wizard seemed to read his mind. "I'll show you," he said, his eyes meeting Tom's.

As Tom watched, a small, flickering flame appeared in the palm of Aduro's upturned hand. Tom gasped as the flame turned violet.

King Hugo looked at Tom through the magical fire, and his eyes

widened. "It cannot be! But...it is.
This is the son of Taladon the Swift!"

# A QUEST

"Taladon!" Tom echoed in shock. "You knew my father, Your Majesty?"

"Oh yes," the king said, smiling. "One of the bravest men I have ever known."

A link with his father at last! Tom felt tears pricking his eyes. The king had seen what Tom had never been able to picture. His father's face.

"Do you know where he is now?" Tom asked, hoping he wasn't being disrespectful.

King Hugo and Aduro exchanged glances. The lords and ladies of the king's council were all listening intently, leaning forward over the dining tables.

The king waved a hand through the air. "It was a long time ago that I knew him..." he said, lifting Tom's chin to get a better look at him. "What is your name, boy?" he asked.

"Tom," the wizard answered for him. "Your Majesty, I must speak with you and Tom alone."

King Hugo nodded to the members of the council. "You may

go. Please treat Edward the page as your honoured guest."

Edward bowed and joined the lords and ladies as they left the room.

As the doors closed, the wizard took the king to one side. Tom strained to catch their conversation as they talked in heated whispers.

At last, King Hugo beckoned to Tom. He approached nervously. What was the king going to say? Was he going to send him away?

"Tom, our land is in terrible danger," said the king. "The Dark Wizard Malvel has hunted down the ancient Beasts and somehow he has gained power over them all.

"The six Beasts have watched

over Avantia and protected us from danger since the first settlers arrived," continued King Hugo, pacing the room. "Ferno the Fire Dragon keeps southern Avantia safe. He makes sure the water supply never dries up. The other Beasts each have their duties, too. But now they have turned against us and carry out terrible acts of destruction in Malvel's name. Even my bravest knights cannot tame them."

"Who is Malvel?" asked Tom.

"Once he was a good man, with a good life," said King Hugo. "But his happiness did not last. He fell victim to that dreadful disease – envy."

Aduro took up the story. "He was

jealous of the Master of the Beasts and his special connection with our kingdom's most powerful creatures. So he searched out forbidden knowledge – wisdom and power dating back to the Dawn of the Beasts."

Tom's mouth felt dry. "And Malvel found that knowledge?"

"Yes. The power that he gained then made him evil, and gave him the strength to break the magical bond between the Master and his Beasts. Ever since, the Master has been imprisoned and Malvel controls the Beasts."

"What do we need to do?" Tom asked.

"Malvel's magic is powerful,"

Aduro said. "Our only hope is that we can find someone with the power to free the Beasts one at a time, and return them to goodness so that they can continue to protect our kingdom rather than ruin it. But," he warned, "we mustn't let our people know the Beasts really exist. These creatures can only do their work if they're left in peace. That's why we've always pretended that the Beasts are not real."

"Malvel has made the Beasts almost unstoppable," the king continued. "Ferno is burning all our crops and blocking up the rivers. And the other Beasts – a sea serpent, a mountain giant, a horse-man, a snow monster and a flame bird – are causing floods, avalanches and chaos elsewhere. They will destroy Avantia unless we set them free from Malvel's wicked enchantment. That is why I sent Sir Caldor to try to unlock the collar that Malvel used to charm the dragon."

He handed Tom a large golden key. "Only this will undo the lock."

Tom slowly turned the key over in the palm of his hand. It was very big, but weighed nothing. He realised it was the key that he'd seen held in Caldor's scorched gauntlet. He looked back up at the king, a question in his eyes.

"The key was created by Aduro," the king murmured, "but must be put to use by a hero. Your father once served me – now I ask you to do the same. Aduro's magic has shown me the strength and honour within you. I'm sure you are a match for any knight in my kingdom." He smiled. "Fate sent you here, Tom. Now I wish to send you on a secret mission…"

A shiver of excitement ran down Tom's spine.

The king leaned forward. "Will you risk your life for the Beast Quest?"

"I will," Tom said without hesitation. He had never been more sure of anything in his life. "Whatever it takes – I *will!*"

# 5

# GATHERING STORM

Tom woke early the next morning.
Where was he? As he looked round
at the big stone windows and the
painting on the wall he suddenly
remembered. He was in the king's
palace, in one of the royal guest
bedrooms! Excited, he jumped out of
bed immediately.

New clothes had been laid out on

a wooden chest near the door. Tom slipped on the dark trousers and woollen, long-sleeved top. Over that he wore a plain blue tunic.

Tom smiled proudly as he looked at his reflection in the mirror. He looked ready for his adventure. Then he felt a moment of doubt.

*Can I really succeed where Avantia's bravest knights have failed?* he wondered.

"Yes, you can," came a soft voice behind him.

With a start, Tom turned to find Aduro at the door. He was holding a sword and a large wooden shield.

"You may think you are an unlikely hero," Aduro went on. "But in strange times, all things are possible."

Tom nodded. "I suppose they are."

Aduro stepped into the room. Slowly, Tom knelt on the cold stone floor before him. He didn't know why, but it felt like the right thing to do. Aduro raised the sword into the air and for a moment Tom could swear that it glowed, lighting up the dust that danced through the air around him.

Aduro and Tom gazed up at the sword, then Aduro brought it down so that the tip of the sword rested gently on Tom's chest, next to his heart. "May this boy have the strength of heart to save Avantia." The wizard's voice rang round the room. Tom bent his head. Then Aduro drew the sword away and gently

pulled Tom to his feet. Smiling,
Aduro held the hilt of the sword out
to Tom. "For you," he said, simply.

Tom took the sword. It fitted his
grip perfectly, and felt far lighter
than the poker he was used to.
"Perfect," he said.

Now Aduro passed him the polished wooden shield. It was well crafted, but very plain. Tom remembered seeing knights occasionally riding through his village with their bright, colourful shields. He couldn't help feeling a twinge of disappointment.

"Appearances can be deceptive," Aduro smiled, again reading Tom's thoughts. "On your Quest you will find allies in the strangest of places, and in the unlikeliest of forms. But you have a wise head, Tom. Trust your instincts. Now, I have other gifts for you." He took a parchment scroll from his pocket. It was just like the one Edward the page had been holding the night before.

As Aduro unrolled it, Tom saw it was a map of Avantia. He stepped forward to get a better look and, as he watched, the map came to life! Trees and hills and mountains rose up from the paper, standing as tall as Tom's thumb. Cautiously, he reached out to touch one of the white mountains in the north. His finger came away glittering with frost.

Tom looked up at Aduro, startled. The wizard nodded at the map.

"Look closer," he commanded.

Now Tom saw tiny, twisting paths spring up like veins on the pale parchment. They slowly spread across the map towards the southwest where a mountain stood, dark and unwelcoming.

"Ferno's mountain," guessed Tom.

"Yes." Aduro held up the golden key Tom had been shown the night before. A loop of leather cord had been threaded through it, and Aduro hung the key around Tom's neck like a medal. "Only if you set Ferno free can we begin to put right Malvel's evil. You must unlock the enchanted collar that imprisons him."

"I will do all I can," Tom promised.

"Now, you must go," Aduro said, handing Tom the map. "Your horse is waiting for you outside."

Tom took his sword and shield and followed Aduro through the palace and out to the stable yard, where a groom stood with a jet-black stallion. At the sight of Aduro,

the horse whinnied in greeting
and tossed his head. It had a white
mark in the shape of an arrowhead
between its eyes, and the brown
leather of its saddle gleamed
brightly.

"The stallion's name is Storm," said
Aduro. "He is young and fast."

Storm pulled away from the groom
and trotted over to them. He pushed
his nose against Tom's shoulder and
gazed at him.

Tom beamed. "I think we'll get
along well, Storm," he said.

Aduro held his sword and shield as
Tom scrambled up onto the horse's
back, then handed them up to him.

Tom looked down at the wizard.
"What will happen to my village,

and my uncle and aunt? They are
relying on me to help."

"A cart is on its way there with
food and water," said Aduro. "The
driver will tell your uncle that you
have been sent on a special errand
for the king – and that you will
return when you can."

Tom patted Storm's neck. "Thank
you, Aduro – and goodbye!"

"Farewell, my young friend. All our
hopes go with you."

Tom nodded and kicked his heels
against Storm's sides.

Storm cantered away, out through
the palace courtyard and into
the hectic city streets, his hooves
clattering on the cobbles as he
swerved round carts and passers-by.

Tom saw the open city gates looming up ahead, and felt his face flush with excitement. Soon he would be on his own. "Faster, Storm!" he urged.

Storm galloped out through the gates, and, as they burst onto the grassy plains outside the city, Tom gave a wild whoop. This was it! His adventure had begun!

Not only was Storm the fastest horse Tom had ever ridden but he also seemed to understand exactly what Tom wanted him to do. He slowed down at the slightest pull on the reins and sped up the second Tom touched his sides with his heels.

By late afternoon they had reached

the southern edge of the grassy plains. A vast forest stretched out before them. It looked dark and mysterious and rather forbidding, but the map showed that the quickest way to the dragon's mountain was to cut straight through the forest.

"Come on, Storm," Tom said, carefully guiding the stallion into the trees. "I think it's this way."

The trail twisted and turned. As they headed deeper into the forest, the trees seemed to get thicker and press in closer. Far above him, the sky was dull, and Tom felt a wave of panic as the gnarled trees and bushes seemed to be reaching out to grab him. Storm's ears flicked as if he sensed Tom's concern.

They carried on until they came
to a small clearing, where the path
seemed to end. Tom dismounted.
Pulling his sword from its sheath,
he started slashing at the dense
undergrowth to clear a way forward.

A rustling sound caught his ear. He stood still and listened.

"Who's there?" Tom called.

There was no answer.

Pressing on, Tom chopped through a thick tangle of brambles. His heart filled with dread. This place

didn't feel right, and now he was
sure that something awful was
watching him.

But taking hold of Storm's reins,
he began pushing his way through
the thicket.

*Graagh!* A set of gleaming, yellow
fangs snapped in his face.

With a shout of alarm, Tom leapt back against Storm. *A wolf!*

Its grey fur was matted, and its amber eyes were wild and staring. Its huge paws were like clubs, and ended in lethal claws. Its teeth were bared in a vicious growl as it prepared to spring!

# THE FOREST OF FEAR

Storm reared up, kicking out with his front hooves, and Tom threw himself into the brambles and bushes. But the wolf didn't attack them. It was growling at something else. Something that was crashing through the undergrowth towards them.

Suddenly, three soldiers smashed

their way into view. Their eyes flashed fiercely through the slits in their helmets. One held a crossbow while the other two waved long swords. The wolf advanced towards them, its growl growing angrier.

"We'll teach that brat and this vermin to steal from our king!" snarled the first soldier, aiming his crossbow at the wolf's head.

"No!" Tom scrambled up from his hiding place – just as the soldier fired an arrow. Without thinking, Tom threw his sword. It spun through the air and sliced the short, heavy arrow in half before plunging into a tree trunk.

"Another poacher! Get him!" One of the soldiers charged at Tom

with his sword raised. But the
wolf threw itself at the man's legs,
knocking them from underneath
him. Outraged, the other two soldiers
charged towards Tom.

Tom grabbed Storm's reins and
swung himself up into the saddle.
Leaning down low, he rushed at the
men with the wolf growling at his
side, sending them running. Pulling
Storm back round, he wrenched his
sword from the tree trunk and rode
towards the soldiers once again,
scattering them into the woods. The
wolf pulled ahead, darting through
the trees onto a narrow path. Tom
and Storm galloped after him.

The wolf moved like the wind,
only slowing once it had led Tom

and Storm a safe distance from the soldiers. Tom eased Storm down to a gentle trot.

Then the wolf stopped, and suddenly, right in front of it, a figure dropped from the trees onto the path. It was a girl.

She was tall and skinny, dressed in breeches and a dirty shirt. Her hair was short and messy, and her face was red with scratches. In one hand she clutched a bow, and in the other a quiver of arrows. As she crouched to greet her wolf, she looked at Tom, her grey eyes narrowing.

"It's all right, I'm not trying to hurt him," he promised as Storm stopped. "My name's Tom," he said, dismounting. "We weren't chasing

him – he was leading us away from
the soldiers."

The wolf padded over to him, and
pushed his nose into Tom's hand.

The girl relaxed and smiled at
him warmly. "Well, Silver seems to

like you and he's a good judge of character. If he trusts you, then so will I."

"How did you get him?" Tom asked, as Silver bounded back to the girl and sat down at her feet, looking adoringly up at her.

"I found him in the woods one day," the girl replied. "Well, he found *me*. I'd got lost, and twisted my ankle. Silver here came along and let me climb onto his back. He carried me all the way home." She stepped forward, took Tom's hand and shook it firmly. "My name's Elenna."

"What are you doing in the middle of the forest?" Tom asked.

Elenna frowned. "My uncle's a fisherman. Silver and I wanted to try our luck on the river. But it's dried up and now we're far from home, with nothing to fish for and nothing to eat." She sighed. "So we came to the forest to hunt rabbits. But the soldiers thought we were trying to steal the king's deer. They chased after us and we got separated."

There was a sudden crash and more shouting behind them. Storm reared and Silver's hackles rose.

"Quick! We'd better get out of here!" said Tom. "They're still coming after us!"

Putting his foot in a stirrup, he swung himself onto Storm's back. Seeing Elenna hesitate, he grabbed her hand and helped her scramble onto the stallion behind him.

Storm leapt forward into a gallop. They raced through the forest, Elenna clinging to Tom, and Silver darting alongside them.

To his relief, the soldiers were no match for Storm's swift hooves. Soon their shouts died away in the distance. Tom drew Storm back to a walk. "I think we're safe," he said, as they reached a small clearing.

Elenna slid down from Storm's back and looked up at Tom. "What's going on?" she asked. "You seem like you're on some kind of mission – but you're too young to be a knight."

Tom hesitated. Something told him he could rely on this girl, and Aduro had told him to trust his feelings. He knew his task was to be kept secret, but perhaps he *could* tell Elenna about his Quest.

"It's the Beasts," he began. "I've been chosen to release them from an evil wizard's spell."

"You?" said Elenna. "But you're just a boy!" She looked hard at Tom. He stared back undaunted. "But I can see why they've chosen you..." she added. Then she raised her eyebrows. "I've always thought the Beasts were more than just a story..."

"They are," Tom told her.

She looked at him, wide-eyed and eager. "So tell me about them."

"They've been turned evil. Ferno the Fire Dragon is under a spell—"

"Ferno?" she gasped.

"He's burning all the crops. And

the river's dried up. If I can't stop him, Avantia will be plunged into famine."

"I knew nothing natural could make an entire river dry up overnight..." Elenna muttered. She bit her lip, then nodded as if she had reached a decision. "I can't let you do this on your own. I'm going to come with you."

Tom grinned. He'd be glad to have a friend by his side as he faced the fire dragon. But then he remembered what had happened to Caldor. "You can't," he said. "It's far too dangerous!"

"Not as dangerous as you doing it all by yourself!" Elenna shot back. She took a step closer. "You saved us from the soldiers. We owe you. Besides..." She hesitated. "There's something special about you. I'd like to help. I *can* help. I know my way around this part of the kingdom. Let me – please."

Tom looked into Elenna's eyes. He knew she meant every word. "What about your family?" he asked.

Elenna shrugged. "My parents died in a fire years ago. My uncle looks after me now."

"I live with my aunt and uncle, too!" Tom said.

Elenna laughed. "I don't know how alert your uncle is, but mine is easily distracted. He probably won't even notice I'm gone for a few days!"

Tom felt a stab of homesickness

as he thought about Errinel, his safe house and his warm bed. Then he pushed the thought out of his mind. He needed to stay strong for the Quest.

"Well," said Elenna. "Can I come?"

"Yes!" Tom said. "I'll be glad of the company."

Elenna let out a whoop of delight. Silver jumped round her legs, barking excitedly.

"So, where do we find this dragon?" she asked, as she calmed the wolf.

Tom patted his pocket. "I have a map to show me," he said quietly. "The big question is – what do we do once we find him?"

# DAWN OF THE DRAGON

Tom, Elenna, Silver and Storm cleared the forest at the end of the first day and were now travelling across rocky ground. They had been travelling without rest for two days and two nights. Desperately tired, they'd camped out last night. They'd all slept heavily, apart from Silver, who had kept an ear out for danger. But morning had soon come, and the fire that had warmed them through the night was dying now. Tom opened the map and studied it.

"Let me look!" cried Elenna, running to kneel next to Tom. Ever since he had first shown her the magical map, Elenna had been fascinated by it.

"We're very close to Ferno's mountain now," he said. "I reckon the Winding River should be near here. But I haven't seen anything."

Elenna pointed through the mist to a massive stack of boulders piled up across the valley below them. "Perhaps the river has been dammed up by all those rocks."

Tom pressed his finger against the river on the map, and, sure enough, it came away bone dry. "I think you're right," he said. "Come on. It's light enough to get moving now."

The sun rose slowly and the mist began to clear. They looked out across the land, at the slope of distant rocky hills and the jagged shapes of far-off mountains. Tom felt a tingle start in his chest and creep through his body. Somewhere out there, his destiny was waiting – and so was Ferno the Fire Dragon.

Later that day they reached the rocky hills. They began to climb and, after a while, arrived at a plateau. The mist was thicker here.

Then suddenly Storm threw back his head and whinnied, and Silver's hackles rose in warning.

"What's got into them?" asked Elenna nervously.

"I don't know." Tom drew his sword and unhooked his shield from his back. Then he walked on alone a little way.

Suddenly, through the mist, a dark shape loomed ahead of him. Tom clutched his sword more firmly as he felt a shiver of anticipation.

But the shape didn't move. Steeling himself, Tom walked a little closer. "It looks like a steep rocky slope," he said. "Slate, I think."

"The animals don't like it," called Elenna.

The key in Tom's pocket began to feel warm. Was it reacting to something close to them, or was he imagining it? "I'm going to explore," he said, looking back at Elenna. "There's something here."

Elenna lifted her bow and pulled out an arrow from her quiver. "I'm coming with you," she said firmly. Tom knew it would be hopeless to argue with her. "Don't even think about leaving me behind," she said, testing the point of the arrow with her thumb.

"I wouldn't dare." Tom smiled, glad she was with him. Then he looked back at the rocky slope, his smile fading. It was time.

Leaving the animals where they were, Tom and Elenna started walking up the slope. The slate was black and glassy, like no rock Tom had seen before. Then he felt a faint vibration under his feet.

"Hold still," he told Elenna. "Something's happening."

They listened, but no – nothing. Only the vibration, pulsing through the rock beneath their feet.

Pulsing like a heartbeat.

Tom crouched to take a closer look at the slates. They seemed to shine like dark scales.

*Scales?*

"Back!" Tom shouted. "Get back to the animals, to the real hill."

Elenna stared at him. "What do you mean, the real hill?"

"This isn't slate," Tom cried, grabbing hold of her hand and pulling her along after him. "*It's dragon skin!*"

Suddenly a terrifying roar rang out around them. Beneath their feet, the ground shifted. They threw themselves off the slope and down to the plateau where Storm and Silver had been pacing anxiously. The wolf howled, while the horse skittered backwards.

Tom had never been so frightened in all his life.

"What are we going to do?" Elenna shouted. "Shall we run?"

Clutching his shield tightly, Tom

tried to think. He was on a Quest
for the king – he couldn't run away
now.

But before Tom could reply, the Beast began to rise from the rocky surface, up and up...

Ferno the Fire Dragon was gigantic. Towering over them all, with his huge, jagged wings extended, he blocked out the sky. His head was coal-black and spiky, and tight around his neck was the enchanted collar, held in place by a golden lock that glowed with a strange, magical light.

Tom gasped. So this was what a Beast looked like! Ferno was as big as a mountain. What chance did a boy have against such a brute?

But as he looked at Elenna standing beside him, bravely clutching her bow and arrow, and as he thought of his friends and family back in Errinel, he knew that however slim his chances, they were worth taking.

"While there's blood in my veins," he vowed, "and for the king and my father, I'll see this through." Just saying the words immediately made him feel braver.

Tom stared up at the dragon as it swung its huge head to and fro above them. "We *must* get that collar off," he said. "That's what is controlling him and making him evil. If we can do that, Ferno will go back to protecting the kingdom instead of destroying it."

Elenna clutched hold of Silver for comfort. "But how will we ever *reach* the collar?" she asked.

Slowly the dragon lowered his head, sniffing the air, his eyes bright and blood-red. His dreadful gaze fell on them. Tom stared deep into the Beast's eyes, mesmerised, and saw himself reflected back in the huge pupils.

Ferno was so close Tom could feel the heat of the dragon's breath on his face. The seconds pulsed by slowly, then Tom snapped out of his trance. With a gulp, he brandished his sword and stood his ground.

Ferno reacted quickly. Uncoiling his huge forked tail, the dragon lashed it out like a deadly whip. But before it could knock Elenna and Tom off their feet, Silver bravely pounced. He snapped his teeth into the scaly flesh at the thin tip of Ferno's tail. With a roar,

Ferno jerked his tail up into the air with Silver still clinging on. The dragon's tail went whistling over Tom and Elenna's heads, whipping Silver through the air. Flung like a

catapulted stone, the wolf landed
with a thump on the rocky ground
and lay still.

"Silver!" cried Elenna, sprinting
towards him.

"No, Elenna!" Tom shouted. "Keep still! Stay there!"

But Ferno had noticed Elenna's sudden movement. He opened his massive jaw, letting out a furious roar. Then he pulled back his head and prepared to strike.

*He's going to attack Elenna!* Tom realised in horror. *She won't stand a chance!*

# 8

# FINAL COMBAT

Tom swung round and whistled to Storm. The jet-black stallion galloped up to him. "Come on, boy," Tom cried, leaping into the saddle. "We've got to save Elenna!"

Tom touched his heels to Storm's sides, and the horse leapt bravely forward. Over the noise of the stallion's pounding hooves, Tom could hear another roar building in the dragon's throat.

"Elenna, look out!" Tom shouted.

Elenna looked round and saw the dragon's huge, open mouth above her. She froze.

As Storm galloped past Elenna and Silver, Tom hurled himself from the horse's back. He landed badly and pain shot through his ankle, but there was no time to stop. There was a boulder on the hillside close by. If they could all just get behind it...

But it was too late.

Ferno's eyes narrowed to fierce slits. With a roar, he blasted an enormous fireball from his mouth. Ignoring the pain in his ankle, Tom threw himself in front of Elenna and held up his shield. The fireball hit the

wooden shield with such force that
Tom staggered back. Flames hissed
angrily round the edges of the shield,
singeing the hairs on Tom's arms as

he struggled to hold it between them and the fireball. The heat burned Tom's throat as he gulped the air, and he could see Elenna's eyes watering, leaving tracks in the dirt on her face. But the shield that Aduro had given him held out – they were safe! The dragon retreated, throwing a final, frustrated hiss over his shoulder. But Tom knew Ferno would return...

Frantically, he threw the shield on the ground to smother the flames, and soon only thick black smoke remained in the air. The shield was scorched, but it was still in one piece. Tom swung it over his shoulder, strapped it into place and helped Elenna up. He could feel her trembling. "Are you all right?"

Elenna nodded her head slowly, her eyes wide in shock. "I think so, thanks to you and Storm. But what about Silver?" The wolf was still lying unconscious on the ground.

"We can't help him until we've dealt with Ferno," Tom told her gently. "If that Beast roasts us, nobody will be left to look after Silver."

"You're right," Elenna said. "But how?"

Tom whistled for Storm. Neighing loudly, the horse trotted up through the curtain of smoke.

"Well done, boy, you were very fast," Tom told him. "But now you've got to be even faster." He scrambled up into the saddle. Then he leaned down and passed his sword to Elenna. "Protect yourself with this."

"What are you going to do?" she asked.

"I'm going to free the dragon!" Tom cried, unfastening his shield and hooking his arm through it, ready for battle. "Wish me luck!" With a whoop, he dug his heels once more into Storm's sides.

The horse shot like an arrow in the direction the dragon had taken.

A few moments later, out of the smoke and mist, Ferno reared up ahead. Hearing Tom and Storm, he turned his huge head towards them. Spreading his wings, he pulled back to strike.

It was now or never. Fighting to

keep his balance, and wincing at
the pain in his ankle, Tom moved
into a crouching position in the
saddle. The horse raced towards
the Beast's outstretched right wing.
At the final moment Storm ducked
to gallop beneath it, and Tom leapt
into the air. With a thump, he landed
on top of Ferno's wing. It felt hard
as stone, but blood-warm. The
dragon flapped his mighty wings
in slow, jerky sweeps. Struggling to
find a handhold, Tom felt himself
start to slip.

With a furious hiss, the dragon
whipped round and thrust his head
up close to look at Tom.

Seizing his chance, Tom dipped
under the Beast's craggy chin and

threw himself at the enchanted collar around its neck.

"Got you!" he cried, slipping his left arm through over the golden edge of the collar. Under here he was safe from the dragon's fire – but now Ferno was throwing his head from side to side, trying to shake him off.

Tom felt as though his arm was about to be torn off, but he gritted his teeth and held on. With his free hand he pulled the key from around his neck and tried to fit it in the lock. But the constant movement of the dragon made it impossible. He tried to steady himself and managed to get the tip of the magic key to the edge of the lock. *Nearly there!*

Ferno roared in anger. The noise

was deafening. Tom's arm burned with pain, and the world started spinning about him. Then, as the dragon flung his head up, the key slipped from Tom's fingers and fell to the ground far below.

"No!" Tom yelled.

The dragon threw his head forward and twisted his neck, but still Tom clung on. He had been so near. So near to victory. But now what could he do to get the key back?

Suddenly, through the drifting smoke, he saw Elenna below, climbing onto Storm. She was holding her bow and arrow, and it looked as if she meant to use it. But she was aiming the arrow at *him!*

"Your shield, Tom!" she yelled.

"What? What are you doing?" he shouted in confusion. Quickly, he shifted his grip on the collar and raised his scorched shield – just as Elenna released the arrow.

With a *thunk* it landed in the scorched wood. Tom peered over the top of the shield.

There was the key. Elenna had found it and tied it to the end of the arrow. *Good old Elenna!* Tom pulled the arrow and the key out of the shield.

The dragon lunged forward and breathed another deadly fireball at Elenna, but Storm was quicker. He thundered over the scorched grass, carrying her clear of danger. The dragon shook his head in fury.

Tom felt his strength return. With the key in his hand, there was still hope!

For an instant the dragon was quiet. Quickly, Tom pushed the key into the lock. It turned with a smooth click.

The enchanted collar glowed a brilliant blue for a moment, then it faded away to nothing.

"I did it!" Tom thought. "I really did it!"

Then, in the same split second, he realised that now, with the collar gone, he had nothing to cling on to but the key. With a shout, Tom found himself plunging towards the ground...

But as Tom fell, the key suddenly rose into the air above him, pulling his arm up. Somehow, it was slowing his fall! He felt the wind rise and carry him over to where Elenna and Storm stood waiting. He landed softly beside them.

"Yes!" he shouted, dazed and jubilant. Ferno had been freed – and it felt as though he had set free something in himself, too. All his doubts and fears of failure melted away. The dragon would threaten the kingdom no longer, and Tom – with the help of his friends – had been the one to put things right.

"Tom, you were almost flying!" gasped Elenna. "How did you do that?"

"It was the key," he said, holding it up in awe.

Just then Silver bounded through the smoke towards them. He was all right! Elenna gathered up the panting wolf in a hug, but her grey eyes were still troubled. "What about Ferno?"

Tom turned to face the Beast. He loomed over them, and Tom had to

lean back to see Ferno's red eyes,
which were still fixed on him. But
this time, Tom wasn't afraid.

"You're free now," he called out
softly. "Free to protect our land and
people."

The fire dragon shook out his
powerful wings. He dipped his huge
head at Tom to acknowledge him and
then he took flight.

Tom and Elenna watched in silence
as Ferno swooped over the dry
riverbed and lashed out with his tail
at the barrier of boulders. The huge
rocks shattered and a wave of clear
water surged down the riverbed like
a caged creature released.

"This was just for starters, Malvel!"
Tom shouted, punching the air. "I

won't rest until *all* the Beasts are free!"

Elenna and Tom could see Ferno drinking deeply from the water of the river. Then he threw back his spiky head, roared, and launched himself into the air, leaving a rainbow of fire across the blue sky. The dragon swooped over Tom and Elenna's heads, and flew towards the horizon. They watched as he disappeared into the distance.

Elenna turned to look at Tom. "How are you feeling?" she asked.

Tom could feel his eyes brimming with happiness. "Like a hero," he replied.

Storm neighed and Silver howled as if they both agreed with him.

Elenna and Tom burst out laughing.

"Now the only question is – what next?" said Tom.

# 9

# THE BEGINNING

"What's that?" Elenna pointed at Tom's pocket.

Something inside was glowing. Light spilled out from Tom's trouser pocket.

Tom quickly reached inside, pulled out the magical map and unrolled it. A puff of silver smoke escaped from the tiny palace marked on the parchment. It rose up before them, growing steadily larger.

Slowly, it started to take shape, and soon Tom could make out the shadowy outline of a man. Two points of silver light sparkled in the cloud of smoke and grew brighter, twinkling merrily, until Tom realised what he was looking at.

"Aduro!" Tom gasped, recognising the twinkling blue eyes of the good wizard. The rest of Aduro took shape in the smoke.

"Well done, Tom," said the wizard. "And you, too, Elenna. Avantia owes you both a great deal."

"How are you doing this?" Tom asked. "How can you see us?"

"Remember the jewel I wear around my neck?" The wizard smiled.

"With that I can see over all the kingdom."

"Then you saw everything that just happened with Ferno?" Elenna asked.

"I did," said the wizard. "And I've told King Hugo about your success. The palace is filled with celebration! You both showed great courage and

determination. You are true heroes.
But are you ready for your next
Quest?"

A tingle crept down Tom's spine.
"The other Beasts have to be freed,
too," he said, excited and nervous all
at once.

Aduro nodded. "But first, Tom,
there is a gift waiting for you."

"A gift? Where?" asked Elenna.

Tom shook his head, baffled. Then
he noticed something glinting in the
scorched branch of a nearby tree.
He looked at Aduro, an unspoken
question in his eyes. Aduro nodded
again, and Tom ran to the tree,
climbing up to retrieve whatever was
caught there.

It was a bluish-black dragon scale,

gleaming like jet. "It's beautiful," he murmured, dropping back down to the ground. "What a souvenir!"

"It is much more than that," said Aduro. "You have earned it by winning your battle with Ferno. Now, if you place it in your shield, it will deflect all kinds of heat!"

Elenna pointed to a scorched groove at the bottom of the shield. As Tom reached out his hand towards it, the groove opened. Tom pressed the scale into place like a jigsaw piece. There was a bright ruby glow and then the wood closed around the edge of the scale, leaving it glinting like a jewel in the light.

"Now, there is no time to waste," Aduro said. "You must follow the path on the map to the next stage of your Beast Quest!"

Tom and Elenna gazed at the map. A snaking green path was starting to form on the parchment, stretching across to the Western Ocean.

"What about our families?" Tom asked. "Can we send a message to them?"

"I'll make sure your families aren't worried," the wizard promised. "But the secrets of your Quest may not be shared with anyone."

"We understand," said Elenna.

Tom thought about his uncle and aunt, and about his father. Not *all* of his family knew Tom had left the village of Erinnel. His father didn't know – wherever he was.

"Now I must leave you," said Aduro. His image began to dissolve like smoke in the breeze. "Good luck, my young friends."

"Wait," said Tom urgently. "What about my father? Will I ever know what happened to him?"

"You will learn a lot on this Quest, Tom," said the wizard, his words echoing into the air. "Farewell..."

The image of Aduro faded. All that was left was a sparkle in the air where the wizard's eyes had been.

Tom looked again at the map. The green path led to a tiny image of a sea serpent, rising up and making splashes with its tail.

He felt his blood chill and his mind darken. He pictured himself struggling in foaming black water against a huge, writhing enemy. He could almost feel great ivory fangs closing down around his body, and sense fierce eyes staring into his soul.

He shook his head quickly and his doubts cleared.

He swung up onto Storm's back. Aduro was right – there was no time to waste. Another Beast had to be set free from Malvel's curse.

Elenna climbed up behind him and Silver trotted alongside, both eager to get going.

Tom pulled his sword out of its scabbard and raised it up, pointing high in the sky.

"Onwards!" he shouted.

Then, returning his sword to its

sheath, he dug his heels into Storm's side and the horse leapt forward. Tom and Elenna were on their way to the next Quest. Tom didn't know what was waiting for him.

But he knew he was ready.

# CONGRATULATIONS, YOU HAVE COMPLETED THIS QUEST!

At the end of each chapter you were awarded a special gold coin.
The QUEST in this book was worth an amazing 10 coins.

Look at the Beast Quest totem picture inside the back cover of this book to see how far you've come in your journey to become

MASTER OF THE BEASTS.

The more books you read,
the more coins you will collect!

Do you want your own
Beast Quest Totem?

1. Cut out and collect the coin below
2. Go to the Beast Quest website
3. Download and print out your totem
4. Add your coin to the totem
www.beastquest.co.uk/totem

*Don't miss the next exciting Beast Quest book, SEPRON THE SEA SERPENT!*

*Read on for a sneak peek...*

# CHAPTER ONE

## SPRINGING THE TRAP

Tom brought Storm to a halt at the foot of a rocky slope. He and Elenna slid to the ground so that the horse could rest. Silver the wolf flopped down beside them, his tongue lolling out as he panted.

The hill where Tom had met and battled Ferno the Fire Dragon was far behind them. Now he and Elenna were heading west on the next stage of their Beast Quest.

Tom's heart began thumping again as he remembered how he had freed Ferno from the curse of Malvel the Dark Wizard. The dragon had burnt crops all over Avantia and blocked the river, making the land dry and barren. When Tom had unlocked the magic collar that imprisoned him, the dragon was released from the spell. As he flew away, he had dislodged the stones damming the river, and a foaming torrent had gushed down the hillside.

"I'll never forget how Ferno broke the rocks with his tail," Elenna said, as if she guessed what Tom was thinking. "Or how you leapt up on his wing! That was really brave."

"It wouldn't have worked if you hadn't shot that arrow up to me, with the key tied to it," Tom replied, feeling embarrassed by Elenna's praise. "I'd never have unlocked the collar without that."

"What you did was still the bravest thing I've ever seen," Elenna insisted.

"We both freed Ferno," Tom said firmly. "And now Avantia has water again."

"Yes, and no more burnt crops,"

Elenna agreed.

Silver leapt up again with an impatient yelp.

Elenna turned to Tom, a determined look in her eyes. "We'd better push on," she said.

Tom could still hear the words of Wizard Aduro ringing in his ears. Freeing Ferno the Fire Dragon was only the first of his tasks. Malvel's curse had turned the Good Beasts of Avantia into evil monsters that were destroying the kingdom. It was Tom's Quest to free all the Beasts and save his people. Tom wasn't sure he could succeed. There was so much he had to do and so many Beasts to conquer! But he meant to try, with all the strength and courage he had.

*While there's blood in my veins,* he thought, *I will not give up.*

This was the adventure Tom had been waiting for all his life. And even though his father, Taladon the Swift, had disappeared when Tom was a baby, he was determined to make him proud.

"Let's have another look at the map," he said.

He pulled out the scroll that Wizard Aduro had given him. On it a path glowed green, winding through hills and woodland until it reached the sea in the west.

As Tom looked at the map, a tiny head reared out of the waves drawn on the paper, just beside a spike of rock that looked like an island. A jagged tail slapped down, sending spray high into the air. Tom started as a drop splashed onto his hand.

"There's Sepron," said Elenna. Her voice was filled with awe.

"I still can't believe it!" said Tom. "A sea serpent!"

"He's angry." Elenna's eyes were wide, as if she had just realised the huge mission facing them. "How do you think he is destroying Avantia?"

"I don't know," Tom said, then he added boldly, "But whatever he's doing, we're going to stop it. That's part of our Quest."

Silver let out another loud yelp. He grabbed the corner of Elenna's cloak in his teeth and tugged gently. At the foot of the slope, Storm scraped one hoof impatiently on the stones.

Tom laughed. "All right, I know. It's time we were going."

He checked the map one last time and stowed it away in his pocket. Before he scrambled back onto Storm, he made sure that the shield Wizard Aduro had given him was firmly strapped to his back. It had been scorched by Ferno, but one of the dragon's bluish-black scales shone in its slot on the shield's surface. Was it true, Tom wondered, that the shield could now protect them from fire?

He swung himself into the saddle. Elenna sprang up behind

him and wrapped her arms round his waist. Tom patted Storm's glossy black neck.

"On to the west!" he cried.

*Read*
*SEPRON THE SEA SERPENT*
*to find out more!*

# FIGHT THE BEASTS,
# FEAR THE MAGIC

Are you a BEAST QUEST mega fan?
Do you want to know about all the latest news,
competitions and books before anyone else?

Then join our Quest Club!

Visit the BEAST QUEST website
and sign up today!

www.beastquest.co.uk

Are you a collector of the
Beast Quest cards?

Go to www.beastquest.co.uk
for more details.

# Discover the new Beast Quest mobile game from

## MINICLIP
## ▶ PLAY GAMES

## Available free on iOS and Android

  amazon.com

Guide Tom on his Quest to free the Good Beasts
of Avantia from Malvel's evil spells.

Battle the Beasts, defeat the minions,
unearth the secrets and collect
rewards as you journey through the
Kingdom of Avantia.

# DOWNLOAD THE APP TO BEGIN
# THE ADVENTURE NOW!